MRS. MAGPIE'S INVENTION

Who invented the nest?

Why, Mrs. Magpie—who else?

And why did she invent it?

For privacy, of course. And for safety too—you wouldn't want to lay your eggs on the ground, now, would you?

Mrs. Magpie invited all the other birds to learn what she had learned, and they all came flying.

But no one ever learns all that a teacher wants to teach them—you know how that is.

Besides, the way some teachers are, Mrs. Magpie was finicky and meticulous.

And, the way some pupils are, hers were inattentive and impatient—to coin a phrase, flighty.

They kept flitting off in all directions, full of ideas of their own and with their lesson half learned.

So now you know—or will, if you half learn the lesson of this charming book—why no two kinds of birds have nests that are alike.

Mrs. Magpie's Invention

WRITTEN & ILLUSTRATED BY

Honoré Guilbeau

YOUNG SCOTT BOOKS

© 1971 by Honoré Guilbeau. All rights reserved. Published by Young Scott Books, a division of the Addison-Wesley Publishing Co., Reading, Mass. 01867. Printed in U.S.A. Library of Congress Catalog Card Number 76-157420. SBN 201-09288-3

Once upon a time, so they say, the birds did not build nests. They laid their eggs on the grass or among the pebbles or on the bare ground.

It was Mrs. Magpie who built the first nest. And I, for one, am not surprised, for she was always collecting ends of strings or shiny stones or odd-shaped twigs. And, of course, sooner or later these had to turn into something.

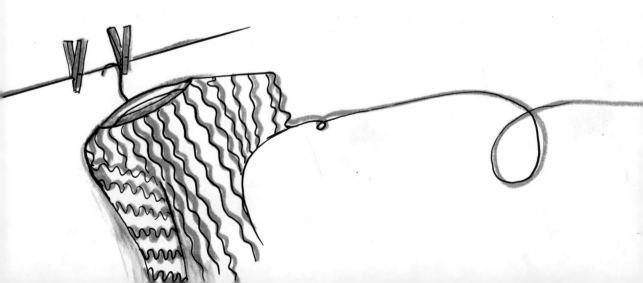

Mrs. Magpie could never say exactly what made her think of building a nest. "It just came to me like that," she said, waving a wing. "And now, of course, I feel that I must share my invention. Think of it! A safe place for eggs! What a boon for birdkind!"

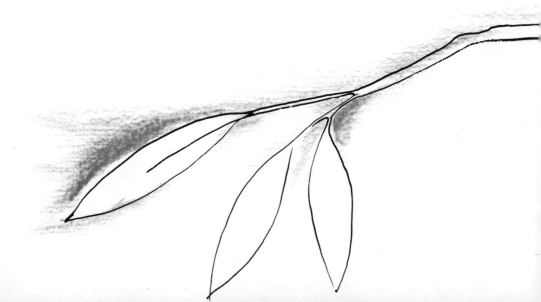

Her cousins, the jays, spread the news. They could be heard everywhere broadcasting loudly to all the birds, inviting them to a lesson on how to build a nest.

"Nest?" said the nighthawk. "I never heard of a nest. What is a nest?"

"Oh," said the jays, all talking at once.

"It's for the eggs, to keep them from being broken . . ."

"It's like a bowl . . ."

"No-o, it's a basket."

"Looked like a lot of sticks to . . ."

"You're all wrong. A nest . . ."

And away flew the jays, still arguing about what a nest was like.

The nighthawk looked after them and shrugged her shoulders. "Nest," she said. "I'm sure my eggs have always hatched out very well. These new things never work, anyway."

So the nighthawk lays her eggs on bare rocks, or on gravelly places, to this very day.

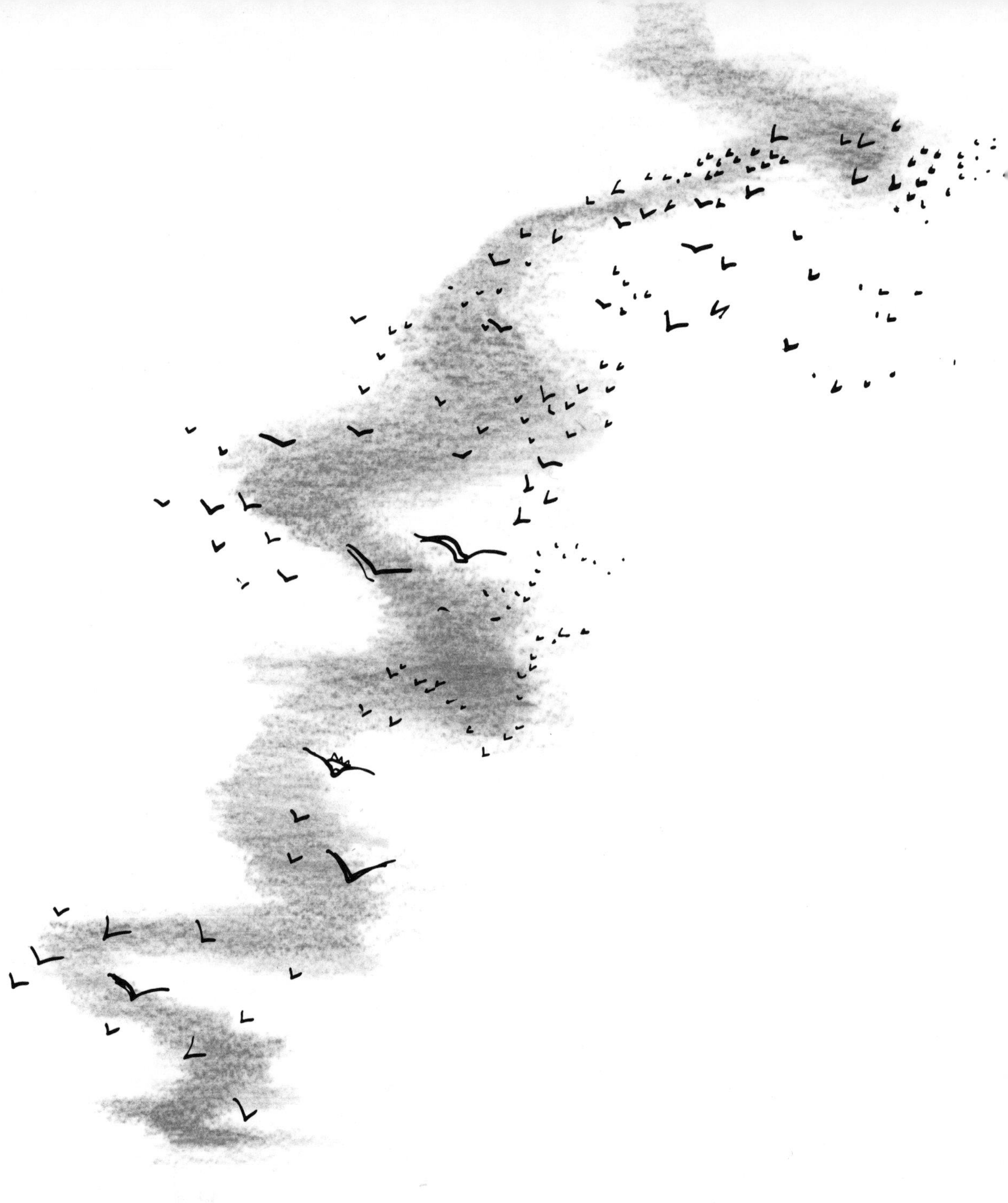

On the appointed day, the birds came to hear
Mrs. Magpie tell about her new invention.

Mrs. Magpie had put her materials close by a
forked branch. She beamed at her audience,
cleared her throat, and began.

"Now then. You take some mud, and you build
a little mound of it." And with her beak, she began
to make a little pile of mud within the fork.

"Well, of course!" said the flamingos, nodding
to each other. "How logical!"

Then without waiting to hear another word,
away they flew to their home in the marshes.

And to this day, flamingos build their nests of mud, piled up above the water level.

"Then you shape the mud—so," continued Mrs. Magpie, using her beak and wings to make a cup shape.

"Oh," said the ovenbird. "Now I know how to build a nest! Nothing to it."

And off she flew to South America.

And to this day, ovenbirds make nests of clay.

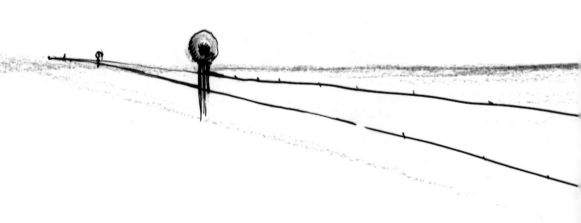

"Next you take some twigs and press them into the mud," said Mrs. Magpie, too busy to notice that her audience was coming and going. "Then push the mud higher and . . ."

"Oh, I can build a nest," said the barn swallow, and away she flew.

Two little owls pushed their way into the place left by the swallows and promptly fell asleep.

"And next, you weave twigs in and out, in and out," continued Mrs. Magpie, using her feet and her beak and adding a dollop of mud here and there to hold the ramshackle mass together.

"Now," she puffed, "take some fine grass, and . . ."

"Grass!" exclaimed Mrs. Oriole to Mr. Oriole. "That's the very thing! Mud! Ugh!"

And off they flew to get some grass.

And to this day, orioles have grass nests that
don't look at all like Mrs. Magpie's.

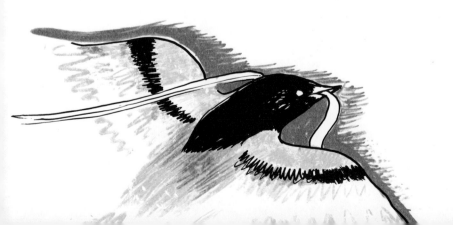

"Now the reason for grass . . ."

At this point the jays began a loud argument about whether corn silk or string might not be better than grass. Then the grackles joined in without really knowing what the fuss was all about, but enjoying it.

Soon they were all wheeling around, shrieking and chattering about goodness-knows-what until nests were forgotten.

"Good riddance," said Mrs. Magpie.

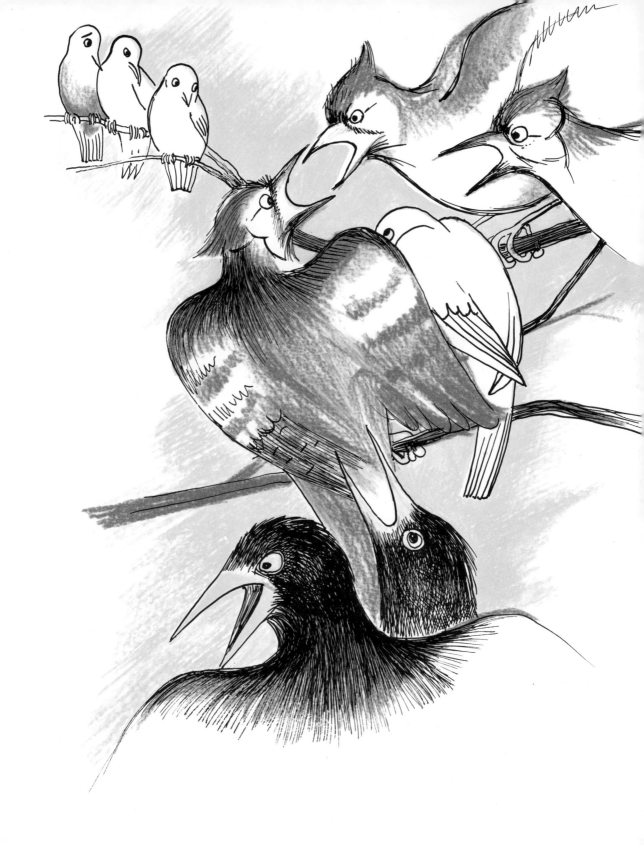

So to this day, their nests look rough and unfinished.

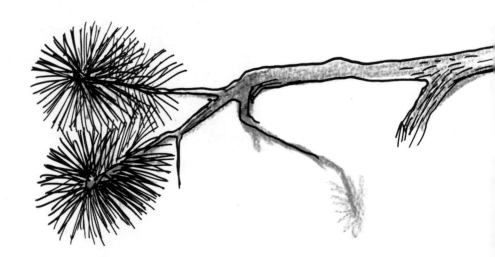

"And fluff from dandelions," continued Mrs. Magpie, "will make it more comfortable." By this time only a robin and the two sleeping owls were left.

"And now for the roof—"

"With leaves above us, who needs a roof?" said the robin, flitting away.

And to this day, robins' nests have no roofs.

"Of course a side entrance is . . ."

That woke the owls and they looked at each other.

"We have a side entrance. I guess we have had a nest all the time."

And the owls flew off silently into the night.

So owls didn't learn to build nests. They just
kept living in hollow trees as they always had.

When the last twig had been arranged to her satisfaction, Mrs. Magpie turned to her audience, expecting loud applause.

There was no one there.

"Well," she said to herself, "I suppose the only real way to learn is to work it out for yourself."

So to this day, no bird builds a nest exactly like any other bird's.

And Mrs. Magpie's nest is one of the most lavish, though not the most beautiful.

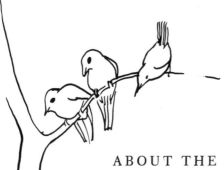

ABOUT THE AUTHOR/ARTIST

Honoré Guilbeau, a native of Baton Rouge, Louisiana, now lives with her husband on a farm in Peninsula, Ohio, but escapes for the winter to Valle de Bravo in Mexico.

Her training at the Art Institute in Chicago was a detailed one, and she has done lithographs and woodcuts as well as murals. In recent years she has been a motive force in a group theater at Peninsula, for which she designs and executes many of the sets and costumes.

Although Mrs. Guilbeau has illustrated three books for the Heritage Press and four children's books for Young Scott Books, this is her first appearance as an author.